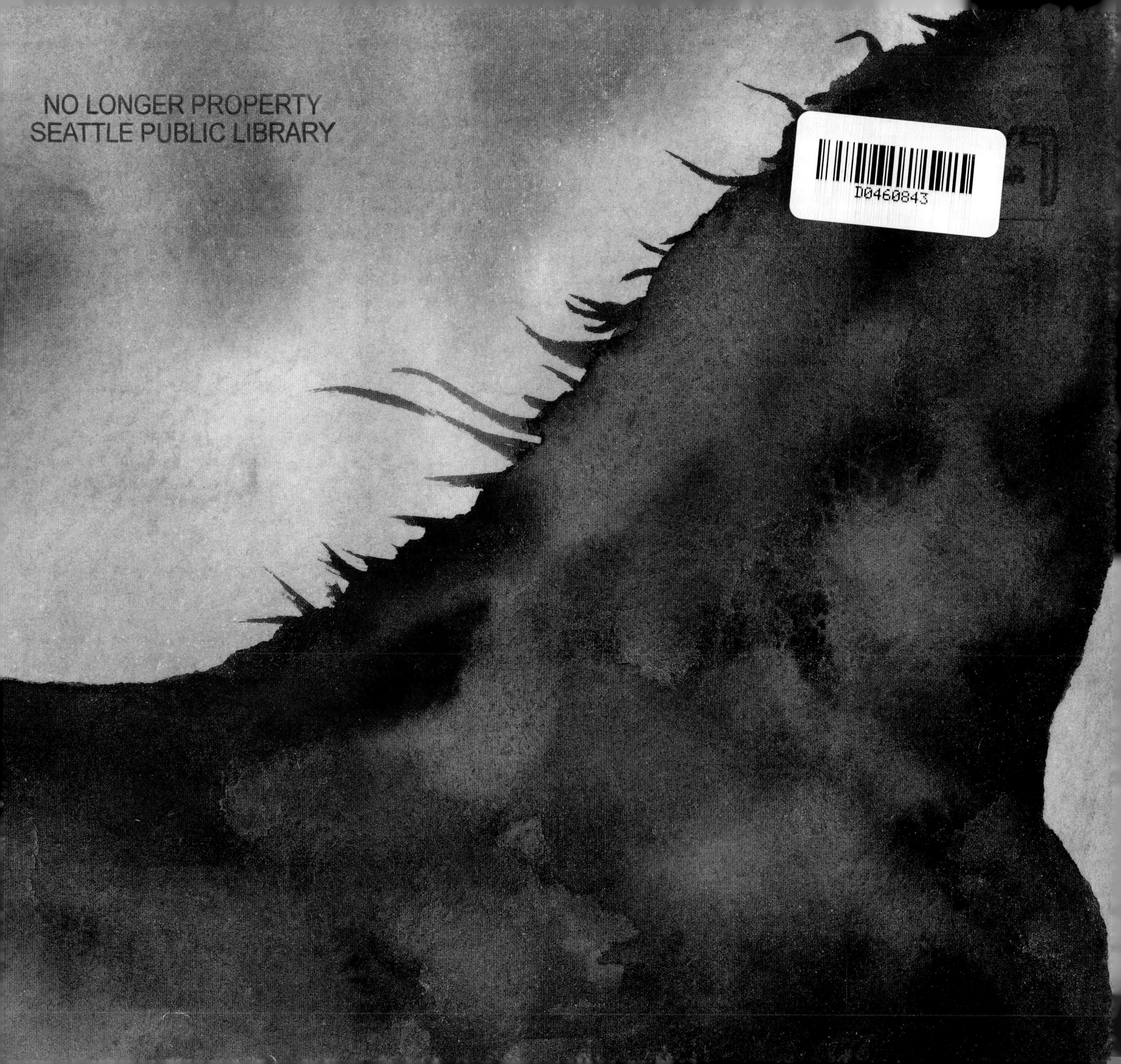

For Wendee and Loraine

Copyright © 2018 by Gianna Marino
A Neal Porter Book
Published by Roaring Brook Press
Roaring Brook Press is a division of Holtzbrinck Publishing Holdings Limited Partnership
175 Fifth Avenue, New York, New York 10010
The artwork for this book was created using gouache.
mackids.com
All rights reserved

Library of Congress Control Number: 2017944655

ISBN: 978-1-62672-908-7

Our books may be purchased in bulk for promotional, educational, or business use. Please
contact your local bookseller or the Macmillan Corporate and Premium Sales Department
at (800) 221-7945 ext. 5442 or by e-mail at MacmillanSpecialMarkets@macmillan.com.

First edition 2018
Printed in China by RR Donnelley Asia Printing Solutions Ltd., Dongguan City, Guangdong Province

1 3 5 7 9 10 8 6 4 2

GIANNA MARINO

If I Had a Horse

A NEAL PORTER BOOK
ROARING BROOK PRESS
NEW YORK

If I had a horse,

I would bring him the biggest apple I could find.

He might be shy.
Like me.

But if I stayed quiet,
he would learn to be
my friend.

If I had a horse, I would hug him . . .

until he let me climb on his back.

At first, I might have to tame him.

And we might not
agree on everything.

I would have to be strong.
Like him.

He would have to be gentle.
Like me.

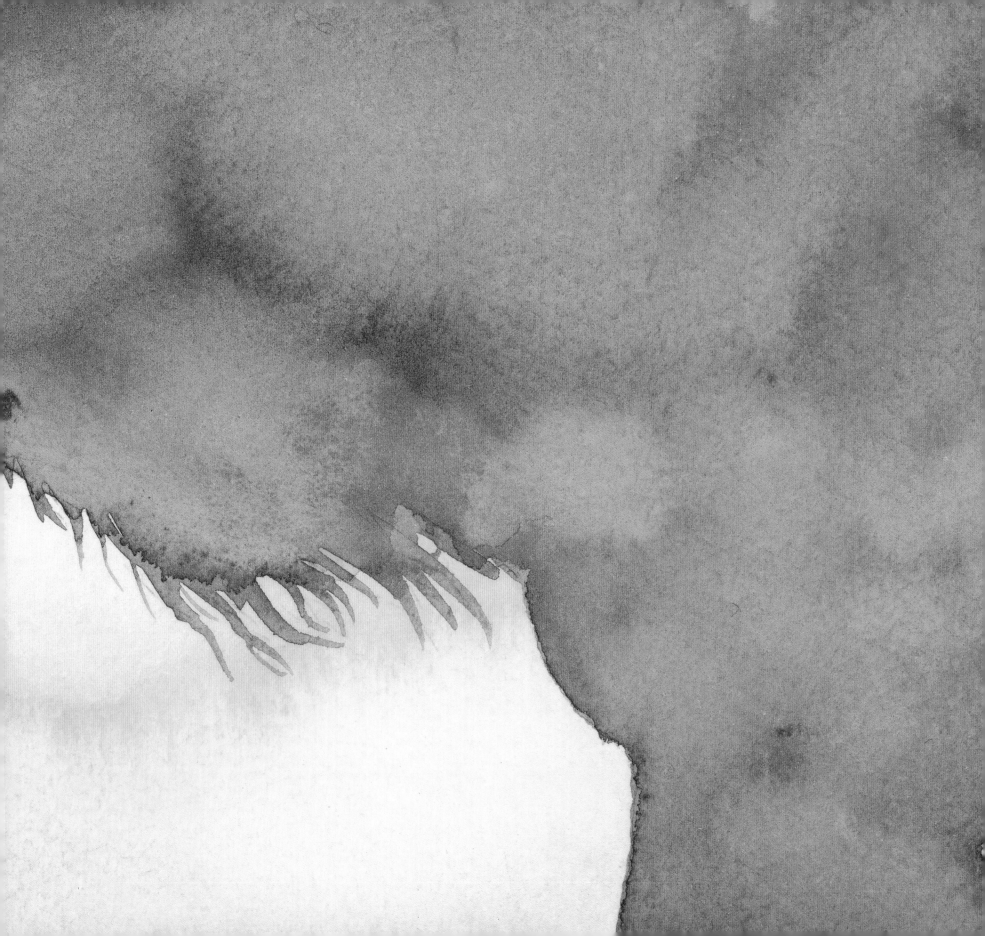

If I had a horse, we would be brave together.

We would explore places we've never been . . .

and run wild
with new friends.

But no other horse
would be like my horse.

If I had a horse,
I would be fearless.
Like him.

And together . . .

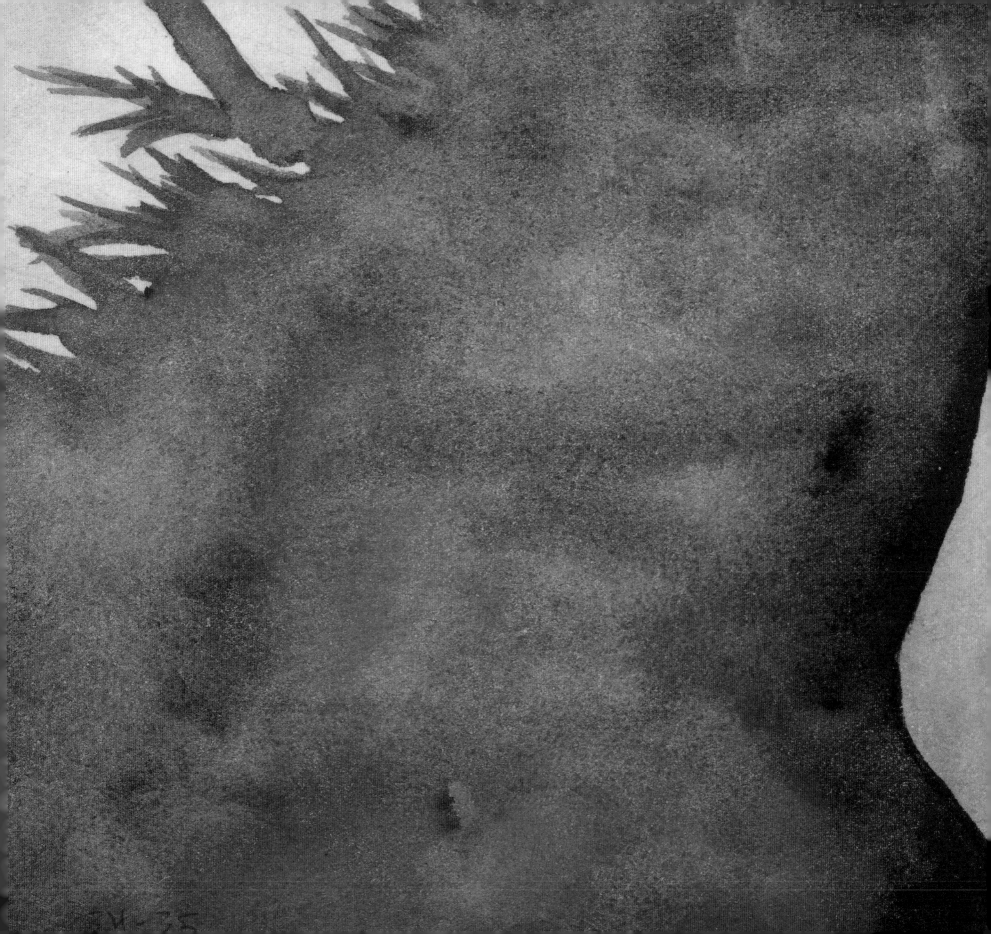

we could do anything.